MARC BROWN

ARTHUR IN A PICKLE

A RED FOX BOOK
Published by Random House Children's Books 20 Vauxhall Bridge Road, London SW1V 2SA
A division of The Random House Group Ltd London Melbourne Sydney Auckland
Johannesburg and agencies throughout the world
Copyright © 1999 Marc Brown
1 3 5 7 9 10 8 6 4 2
First published in the United States of America by Random House Inc and
simultaneously in Canada by Random House of Canada 1999
First published in Great Britain by Red Fox 1999
All rights reserved.
Printed in Hong Kong by Midas Printing Limited
THE RANDOM HOUSE GROUP Limited Reg. No. 954009
ISBN 0 09 940405 2

Red Fox

The school bell rang.

"Time to hand in your homework,"
said Mr Ratburn.

Everyone did — but Arthur.

"Where is your homework?"
Mr Ratburn asked Arthur.

"My dog ate it," said Arthur.
"I don't think so,"
said Mr Ratburn.
"Go to the headteacher's office
first thing in the morning.
You're in a pickle now, Arthur."

That night, Arthur just played
with his food.

He tossed and turned in bed.
"I'm in a pickle," he said again
and again until he fell asleep.

He dreamed that
the pickle police
were chasing him!

He jumped into his pickle car.
He stepped on the accelerator —
but he didn't get far.

The pickle police said,
"Take him away!"

Up in the sky, a pickle plane
flew through pickle snow
and rain.

The pilot threw down a rope
and pulled Arthur up.

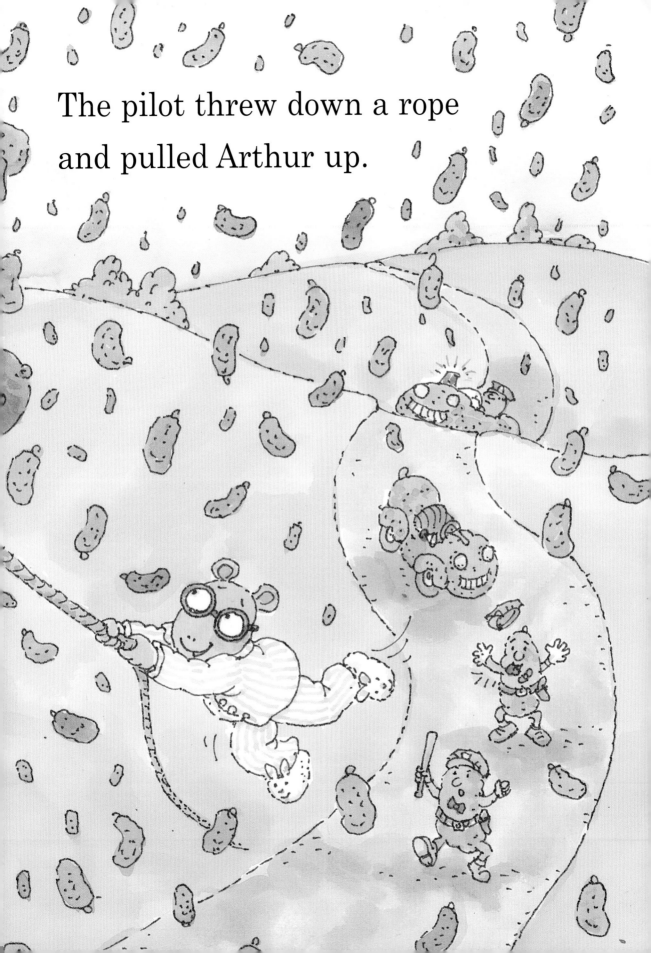

The plane landed in
Pickletown.

"Look!" said D.W. "A pickle steeple!"

"Look!" said Arthur. "Pickle people!"

Some had pickle hair.

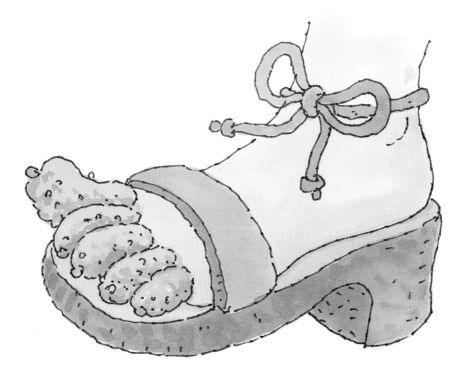

Some had pickle toes.

Some a pickle ear.

Some a pickle nose.

"Didn't do his homework!" said Pickle Nose. "Lied that he did!" said Pickle Toes.

"You're going to jail —
and absolutely no bail!"
shouted Judge Picklepuss.

The jailer put Arthur
on a pickle diet,
and every day he said,
"Just try it."

For breakfast, pickle doughnuts and pickle flakes...

For lunch, pickle pie and pickle shakes...

For dinner, pickle soup and pickle cakes.

"Let me out!
Don't be so mean.
I've had it," moaned Arthur.
"I'm turning green."

Suddenly, Arthur woke up.
He went to his desk,
opened his book,
and did his homework.

At school, Arthur went right
to the headteacher's office.
"I cannot tell a lie," he said.
"My dog did not eat
my homework.
I did not do my homework.
But it is here now.
I'm sorry."
The headteacher smiled.
"Well, thank you, Arthur,"
he said.

Arthur felt great all day —
until he asked,
"What's for dinner?"
and Dad said,
"Pickled cabbage!"